WELCOME TO
ISRAEL
The Holy Land

TABLE OF CONTENTS

Places to Go 4–15

Sights to See 16–25

Culture to Experience 26–37

People to Know 38–41

Curiosities to Consider 42–47

Words to Work On 48

MAP OF ISRAEL

Hop in a car to zip across Israel, from east to west, in about the same time it takes to watch a movie. You could watch six movies in the time it takes to drive the length of Israel from north to south.

Where in the world is Israel?

EUROPE

ASIA

AFRICA

Suez Canal

PLAINLY POPULAR

Little and Lush

The coastal plain of Israel is a strip of land along the Mediterranean Sea and is so narrow a marathoner could run across it. More than half of Israel's population lives in this region.

© David Ionut/Shutterstock

The Coastal Plain
is only 116 miles long.

© Duby Tal/Albatross/age fotostock

First-Class Dirt

© ZUMA Press, Inc./Alamy

Israel includes busy cities, sandy beaches, and rich farmland. Heavy dark soil helps crops such as wheat and hay grow. Thinner, sandier soil is great for growing citrus fruits like oranges, grapefruits, and tangerines.

"The City That Never Sleeps"

A modern center for business and performing arts, **Tel Aviv** attracts tons of visitors and VIPs and gets its nickname because of the constant activity in the city. In 1950, Tel Aviv merged with nearby Yafo. One of the oldest port cities on earth, Yafo was called Joppa or Jaffa in the Bible. Jonah boarded a boat here before he bumped into a very big fish (Jonah 1:3).

© Dmitry Pistrov/Shutterstock

Long History

Haifa rests on the slopes of **Mount Carmel** where Elijah showed some false prophets who was boss (Answer: God. See 1 Kings 18). Haifa has been governed by ten different countries in the last 3,000 years.

© Baker Photo Archive

WIDE RANGE

Lotz o' Kibbutz

The **Jezreel Valley** contains Israel's richest farmland which is cultivated mostly by organized communities that all work with each other called *kibbutzim* or *moshavim*.

Tip Top

Not all mountains are created equal. Cliffs in northern Israel settle into rolling hills in Samaria. Golan Heights has the country's only **basalt** (lava that cooled and hardened quickly). And Judea has rocky hilltops, olive trees, and terraced hillsides.

Mountain Ranges
Volcanoes formed the steep cliffs in Golan Heights.

8

Old and Honored

More people live in Jerusalem than in any other city in Israel. Today, Jerusalem's borders include a bigger area than the Old City, which is recognized as a World Heritage Site—a place having special cultural significance.

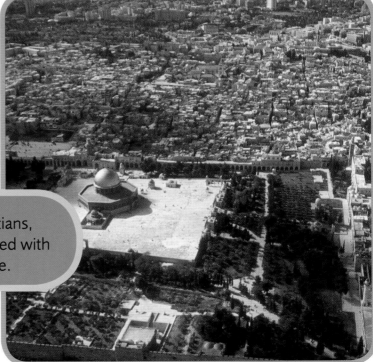

A holy city to Jews, Christians, and Muslims alike, Jerusalem is filled with ancient history and modern culture.

THROUGH THE HULA

Crack Up

The green, flowering Hula Valley is part of the Great Rift Valley, a huge trench in the earth's crust that runs through Israel for a total of 4,000 miles. The narrow **Jordan River** flows down the Hula Valley into the Dead Sea.

Hula Valley
Popular stop for birds (and the people who watch them).

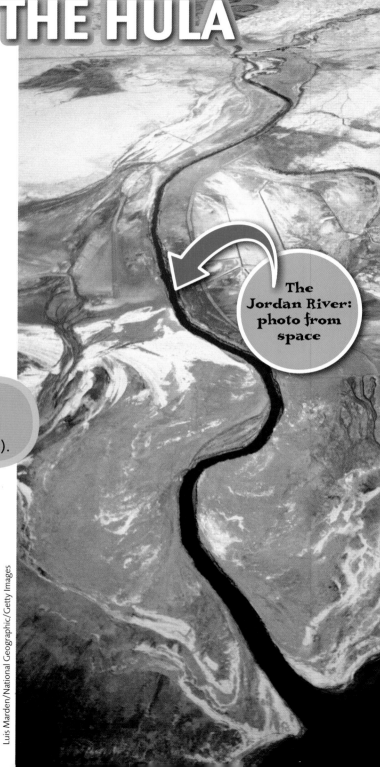

The Jordan River: photo from space

© xpixel/Shutterstock

Luis Marden/National Geographic/Getty Images

HOT DIGGITY

The Arabah
Death Valley in California averages more rainfall every year than this region.

רכיית ישיבא ר"ד:/Wikimedia Commons, CC-BY 2.5

Dead Sea to Red Sea

The Arabah, Israel's long eastern valley, gets very little rain throughout the year. Still, farmers have been able to develop efficient systems for nourishing plants, controlling water, and successfully harvesting dates, figs, tomatoes, melons, peppers, and more.

Problem Solving

The Arava Institute for Environmental Studies researches environmental problems in the Middle East and explores ways to solve them. College students stay at Kibbutz Ketur to study things like water management and farming methods.

Ed Kashi/National Geographic Creative

HIGH AND DRY

Toasty Terra Firma

The Negev is a desert region in southern Israel with rocky canyons, sandstone hills, sharp cliffs, and dry riverbeds called *wadis*. Three distinct box canyons called *makhteshim* also dot the desert. The biggest *makhteshim* is five miles across and 21 miles long (more square miles than Washington D.C.).

Wikimedia Commons

Baker Photo Archive

More Fields than Folks

Although the Negev includes more than half of Israel's land mass, more people actually live in the city of Jerusalem. Israel Defense Forces are based in the Negev alongside **Bedouin villages**. You might have heard of one famous resident: Abraham.

Ester Inbar/Wikimedia Commons

Seaside City

In the Bible, when Moses led the Israelites out of Egypt, they crossed the Red Sea and camped around **Eilat**. Over 400 years later, King David took over the port city when he conquered Edom. Today, there's a lot less camping and conquering and a lot more vacationing, snorkeling, diving, and bird watching in Eilat.

The Negev

Negev comes from a Hebrew root word meaning 'dry.' In the Bible it was used to mean the direction 'south.'

WATER WAYS

© ProfStocker/Shutterstock

Pass the Salt

The lowest point on earth is here in Israel and contains the sea with the saltiest water on earth. The **Dead Sea** is not the spot to refill your water bottle, but if you want to float without even trying, this sea is the place to be.

Freshen Up

Jesus started calling his disciples at the Sea of Galilee, now called **Kinneret** (Matthew 4:18). The Jordan River and underground springs fill this lake with fresh water.

Jesus Knew the Jordan

By the time the narrow **Jordan River** hits the Dead Sea it has traveled 186 miles and dropped more than 2,300 feet. In the 1950s the river was diverted. This means people worked to change the direction the river was flowing. The move preserved drinking water but seriously lowered the Dead Sea's water level.

Gulf Club

Israel meets the Red Sea at the **Gulf of Eilat**. The deep blue water is home to a coral reef and sea creatures of all shapes and sizes. Divers can see many marine fish, beautiful coral, and some interesting shipwrecks as they explore.

Cool Caves

Western Israel lies next to the Mediterranean Sea. In the north, at **Rosh HaNikra**, the water has worn away parts of white chalk cliffs and formed amazing natural caves called *grottoes*.

NORTHERN SIGHTS

Up and Down

An area of rugged natural beauty, **Golan Heights** is filled with wide views and wildlife. Water falls into canyons, eagles soar to high nests, and ruins of settlements go back thousands of years and bring thousands of tourists to the area.

© Blaze986/Shutterstock

Rock It

During his ministry, Jesus led his disciples as far north as Caesarea Philippi near the **Banias Spring** that still flows today. Long ago water poured from the bedrock of a cave and made its way to the Jordan River. Near there, Jesus changed the name of his apostle Simon to Peter, which means "the rock." "And I tell you that you are Peter and on this rock I will build my church ..." (Matthew 16:18)

Jesus also said,
"Whoever believes in me, as Scripture has said, rivers of living water will flow from within them" (John 7:38).

Jesus Was Here

Much of the rocky region in northern Israel is in the province of Galilee. Natural sights and man-made ruins make Jesus' stomping grounds worth discovering.

WATER WORLD

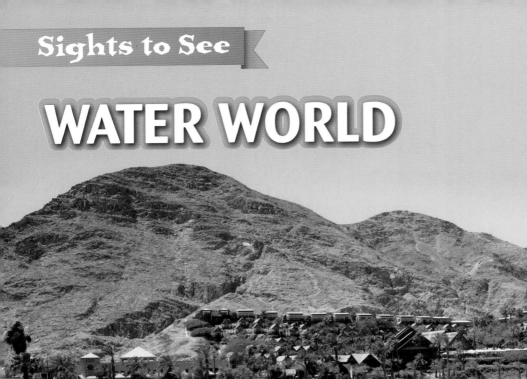

Pass It On

At the Gulf of Eilat, the sheltered water makes a great habitat for different species of coral. In turn, **coral reefs** make great habitats for sea plants and animals. Not only does the coral offer fish some fine dining, the little swimmers can eat in peace, sheltered from danger.

Beyond the Beach

Perhaps more than 1,200 species of fish live in the area of the Gulf of Eilat—**flat butterfly fish**, bony varieties, slim ones of silver, and flashy ones of crazy color—zip around leaving experts to count and identify them all.

© Vlad61/Shutterstock

Danger in the Deep

Even in the cool, clear waters of the gulf, sea life is threatened. Coral reef communities remain under stress from people and pollutants. Even nature itself threatens the reef communities. For example, beautiful **lionfish** can disrupt the neighborhood. They tend to move in, make themselves comfortable, and take over a delicately balanced area.

© frantisekhojdysz/Shutterstock

Stay Dry Under Water

Visitors to the Gulf of Eilat can see the sea up close and personal with snorkels and flippers. Or they can check out the views from the **Coral World Underwater Observatory**. The distinctive white tower of the observatory marks the glassed-in view 20 feet beneath the surface of the Red Sea.

© Eitan Simanor/Alamy

Sights to See

IN THE BANK

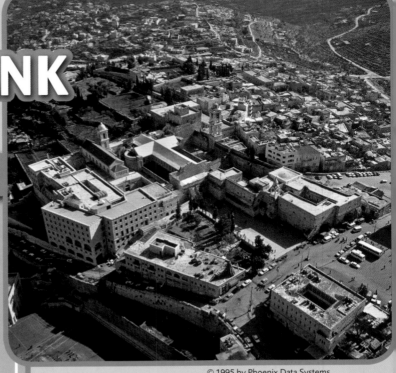

© 1995 by Phoenix Data Systems

Common Ground

On the right side of a map of Israel is a section of land referred to as the **West Bank**. This area is filled with a whole lot of people, diverse churches, and historical sites that are important to three very different faiths— Judaism, Christianity, and Islam.

Saved Cave

The **Church of the Nativity**, in Bethlehem, is the oldest surviving Christian church in the world. Some believe it marks the spot where Jesus was born. St. Jerome spent 30 years in a cave beneath this church translating the Bible into Latin.

www.HolyLandPhotos.org

That's Deep

In John 4, Jesus offered "living water" to a thirsty Samaritan woman at a well. Many people insist this happened at a place in the West Bank now called **Jacob's Well**—after all, it's tough to simply move a hole that is more than 100 feet deep.

Set in Stone

In John 11, Jesus miraculously raises his friend Lazarus from the dead. Today visitors can descend the stone stairs into Lazarus' tomb in **Bethany**, a two-mile walk from Jerusalem.

HEROD THE (NOT SO) GREAT

Stay on Top

Many huge compounds were built by the king of Judea, Herod the Great. (Really, that's what he was called!) For **Herodium**, his desert fortress, Herod had the top of a mountain flattened to make room for a seven-story palace, stables, and a pool big and deep enough for boats.

From his view at **Herodium**, Herod could see Bethlehem where a greater king, the King of kings, had just been born. Herod didn't know exactly where Jesus was, so he desperately ordered every boy younger than two in the town to be killed (Matthew 2:16). But Jesus and his family escaped to Egypt until Herod was buried in his huge palace that now lies in ruins.

Can't Touch This

To escape his enemies, Herod built a massive fortress on top of a high plateau surrounded by sheer cliffs. The ruins at **Masada** show three levels, a grand palace, watch towers, and a double wall for protection.

Michael Melford/National Geographic/
Getty Images

Peter and Paul Stayed Here

Caesarea, located on the Mediterranean Sea halfway between Tel Aviv and Haifa, served as the largest port city of Herod's kingdom. Today, visitors can glimpse the grandeur of the ancient city named after a ruler called Augustus Caesar—the ruins of ancient theaters, Herod's huge palace, and the broad steps that lead from the pier to the ancient temple.

Baker Photo Archive

SOUTH SEE

Old Town

Ancient ruins at **Be'er Sheva** show a settlement of early Israelites who lived 1,000 years before Christ was born. It is believed that Abraham and his son Isaac lived in this city for many years (Genesis 22:19). As part of the first planned community in the area, streets were laid out and a huge container for water was carved out of the rock beneath the settlement.

Sand and Stone

The barren beauty of **Timna Valley National Park** in southern Israel features ancient Egyptian copper mines, grand sandstone formations, and a cliff wall with chariot carvings showing Egyptian warriors holding shields and axes.

Perfect Hiding Spot

David found the perfect hiding place from Saul and hid near the desert oasis of **Ein Gedi**, near the Dead Sea. King Saul pursued him where wild goats climb craggy rocks (1 Samuel 24:2). Springs provide water year round in the nature preserve that features animals and plants unique to Israel and the surrounding countries.

Todd Bolen/www.BiblePlaces.com

© Vladimir Blinov/www.123RF.com

© 1995 by Phoenix Data Systems

IN GOOD FAITH

© Kobby Dagan/Shutterstock

Better Believe It

Religion has played a major role in Israel's ancient history and current culture. If you randomly gathered 100 residents from all over Israel, 75 would be Jewish, 17 would be Muslim, and two would be Christian.

Father Abraham

Although they maintain very different beliefs, Judaism, Christianity, and Islam trace their religions back through Abraham. God told Abraham: "I will surely bless you and make your descendants as numerous as the stars in the sky and as the sand on the seashore" (Genesis 22:17).

© Providence Collection/GoodSalt

Same Difference

Jews believe Israel is part of their geographical history and they, and the land, have sacred ties to God as his chosen people. Muslims believe the Prophet Mohammed went to heaven from Jerusalem's **Dome of the Rock** in Jerusalem. For Christians, Jesus' ministry—and the ministry of his followers after him—started in the Holy Land as well.

© Martin Froyda/ Shutterstock

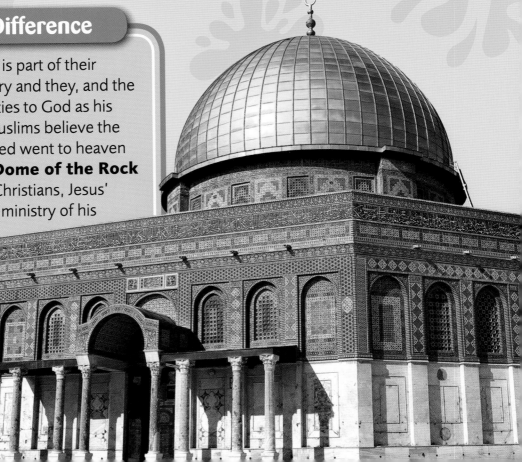

DAY BY DAY

Keep in Mind

Between national holidays and religious observations in Israel, it's almost hard to keep track of special days. For example, there are three different "days of rest"—Fridays for Muslims, Saturdays for Jews, and Sundays for Christians.

B. Anthony Stewart/National Geographic/Getty Images

© silver-john/Shutterstock

Time Out

On Friday afternoons, shops, offices, and certain restaurants close in the afternoon to prepare for Shabbat (the Jewish Sabbath), which begins at sunset. The restaurants don't reopen until Saturday evening after dark.

On Schedule

Israel is the only country in the world where most of the citizens are Jewish. So the following days are worth celebrating:

HOLIDAY	WHAT IS CELEBRATED	WHEN
Rosh HaShanah  © Howard Sandler/Shutterstock	The Jewish New Year	From 1st day of Tishrei (7th month in Jewish calendar) lasting 2 days (September)
Yom Kippur  © GWImages/Shutterstock	Day of Atonement—the most holy day of the year for Jewish people everywhere	10th day of the month of Tishrei (September)
Passover  © grafnata/Shutterstock	A time to celebrate the deliverance of the Jewish people from slavery in Egypt	Early spring— from the 15th –22nd in the Jewish month of Nisan
Independence Day  © Sokolovsky/Shutterstock	A holiday celebrating Israel's declaration of independence in 1948	5th day in the Jewish month of Iyar (April)

GOOD ENOUGH TO EAT

Spice Is Nice

The Palestinian zatar is a traditional mix of local spices that can include the dried, bitter, minty leaves of the hyssop plant. Zatar is used as a dip for bread (like a pita), a spread when mixed with olive oil, and as a seasoning for meats and vegetables. A wallet filled with Israeli shekels can buy food and the zatar spices at open air markets called *souks*.

© Art of Food / Alamy

Diet du Jour

© Neil A Rodrigues/Shutterstock

To order off a menu, you'll need to know the language of Israel:

falafel—fast food made of fried chickpeas and formed into a patty

sahlab—sweet milky drink usually served warm

shawarma—meat, sesame seed sauce, and salad tucked into a pita

© sowar online/Shutterstock

© Art of Food / Alamy

© MSPhotographic/Shutterstock

Made to Order

Many Jewish people eat according to special religious laws spelled out in the Kashrut. Called "kosher" in English, this means skipping foods such as pork and shellfish. It also means foods must often be made a certain way. Since many Jews observe these laws, kosher food and restaurants are easy to find all over Israel.

A

Can You Name These Fruit?

Just like in many other countries there are foods that are not familiar to everyone in the world. Maybe you haven't heard of fruit like litchi, dates, guava, or pomelo. Can you name these foods grown in Israel?

B

D

C

© vlad09/Shutterstock
© Valentyn Volkov/Shutterstock
© ANCH/Shutterstock
© Art of Food / Alamy

31

ANSWERS: **A.** pomelo; **B.** guava; **C.** dates; **D.** litchi

GOOD SPORTS

Fun and Games

Since 1932, the **Maccabiah Games** have brought athletes to Israel from all over the world. Starting at age 15, Israeli citizens and Jewish athletes who qualify can compete every four years in events like fencing, cricket, chess, softball, basketball, and wrestling. In 2009, Israel hosted athletes from 51 countries to compete in 31 events.

Nir Elias/Reuters /Landov

Tsafrir Abayov/AP Images

Dive In

Because Israel has easy access to seas and harbors, water sports are popular pastimes. Sailing, kayaking, windsurfing, and diving are sports people participate in both for fun and competition. Half of the country swims several times a year in one of the hundreds of community pools.

MACCABIAH GAMES

First Things First

In the 1988 Olympics, athletes Eitan Friedlander and Shimshon Brockman chose not to compete on Yom Kippur (the holiest day of the Jewish year). Choosing to respect their faith, they forfeited that day's race and finished fourth, one place behind an Olympic medal that would have been Israel's first.

COLOR AND MELODY

© Israelimages

Heart for Art

About 100 years ago, the **Bezalel Academy of Art and Design** was established in Jerusalem. (Exodus 31 names Bezalel as the chief artist of the tabernacle.) At first, traditional Jewish and biblical art was all the rage. Little by little Hebrew artists branched out to other themes at the academy.

Show Off

Many galleries throughout the country display Israeli art. There are more museums per person in Israel than in any other country on earth.

© Pavel Bernshtam/Shutterstock

© Robert Harding World Imagery / Alamy

Watch Out

About 400 pieces of art are randomly sprinkled in public places around Israel. You might see a mosaic mural, a sculpture of a rabbit made of rusted iron, a smooth boat sculpted out of volcanic rock from Galilee, or a bronze statue of a couple lying in a sardine can.

Fine Tune

Music lovers can tune in to six different orchestras including the Jerusalem Symphony Orchestra (every concert is recorded and then broadcasted). The **Israel Philharmonic Orchestra** has been Israel's national orchestra since it started as the Palestine Philharmonic Orchestra in 1936.

Paul Hurschmann/AP Images

35

SUPER SCIENCE

© Protasov AN/Shutterstock

Good Moves

Much of Israel is hot, dry desert. Scientists have taken special interest in developments that help their land and people in practical ways.

Put to the Test

Many Israeli universities are recognized as top schools in the world in subjects like math, physics, and computer science. Since 2002, Israel has produced six Nobel Prize-winning scientists in chemistry and economics. Dan Shectman and Ada Yonath are two of these amazing scientists.

Technion, Israel Institute of Technology/Flickr, CC BY-SA 2.0

ISRAEL LEADS THE WAY IN ...

© Eldad Carin/www.istockphoto.com

© ChameleonsEye/Shutterstock

... harnessing power from the sun. Over 90 percent of Israeli homes use solar power for hot water. (That's the highest percentage in the world.)

... growing food in tough conditions. Scientists explore greenhouses and new seeds that grow better than before.

© PhotoStock-Israel / Alamy

... improving farming. Upgraded systems make it faster and easier to feed herds, milk cows, and collect eggs.

... managing water. Agricultural experts developed revolutionary drip systems to water crops in huge areas as well as on small farms. This means water can be saved, channeled, and used a little at a time.

FIRST AND FOREMOST

First Prime Minister

When Israel became an independent nation, **David Ben-Gurion** became the first prime minister. After six years of service, he took a break and then returned to office to become the third prime minister as well.

Keystone/Hulton Archive/Getty Images

First Woman Prime Minister

Golda Meir served as the first woman prime minister. Many years before she was elected, she joined a kibbutz in the Jezreel Valley where her responsibilities included picking almonds and working in the chicken coops.

Hulton Archive/Getty Images

Max Nash/AP Images

First Nobel Peace Prize

Menachem Begin was the first of three Israeli prime ministers to win the Nobel Peace Prize, an award given for outstanding contributions to peace.

NASA

First Astronaut

Fighter pilot **Ilan Ramon** became the first Israeli astronaut when the space shuttle Columbia took flight. In 2003, after more than two weeks in space, the shuttle tragically broke apart at re-entry. The diary he kept on the journey miraculously survived the accident. It was returned to his wife who donated it to Jerusalem's Israel Museum.

Press Association via AP Images

First Olympic Medal

In 1992, Israel took home its first Olympic medal ever when **Yael Arad** won silver in women's judo. A day later, Oren Smadja won the country's second medal, also in judo.

FACES IN THE CROWD

State Rules

Israel's basic laws declare it a Jewish and democratic state. "Star of David," also known as the Shield of David, is a symbol of Jewish identity. It recognizes King David of the Bible.

© Sokolovsky/Shutterstock

Gather Together

Most people in Israel live in cities. A small number of people live in cooperative settlements or small desert communities similar to the kibbutz.

© Geothea/Shutterstock

Bedouin: After being adopted by an Egyptian princess and raised as royalty, Moses lived for a time like a nomadic Bedouin, tending sheep in the desert wilderness.

Heard the Word

Israel's official languages are Hebrew and Arabic, but English is widely used too. Because so many people from other countries (like Russia, Finland, and Armenia) moved to Israel, other languages and cultures have mixed in as well.

Grow Up

When the state of Israel was established in 1948, there were less than a million people living there. A year later Israel's population reached a million citizens. Almost ten years later, its population doubled.

© Nir Levy/Shutterstock

PhotoDisc

BIRDS OF A FEATHER

© Protasov AN/Shutterstock

Bird's Eye View

More than 500 million birds pass over the country of Israel each year to follow warm weather. These regular migration patterns make Israel a paradise for bird watchers (and a headache for pilots).

Wing It

More than 500 different species of birds call Israel home, from cranes and ducks to parakeets and wheatears. One hundred forty species are rare. Fourteen are globally threatened.

© Vladimir Kogan Michael/Shutterstock

Pecking Order

Israel hosts eagles that hunt during the day, owls that stay up all night, **ostriches** that couldn't fly if they wanted to, loons that spend more time in the water than the air, big albatrosses that soar with wide wingspans, and little storm petrels that flutter like bats.

© Sergei25/Shutterstock

Rule the Roost

A **hoopoe's** call—oop-oop-oop—sounds a lot like its name. During Israel's 60th anniversary, the hoopoe was voted the official national bird. Referred to as "mountain chiseler," the sharp-beaked hoopoe can cut through stone (according to legend anyway).

© Panu Ruangjan/Shutterstock

Funny Bunch

Busy birds like honey buzzards, oystercatchers, bee eaters, king fishers, and Old World warblers land in the Holy Land.

© Alexander Sviridenkov/Shutterstock

43

FANTASTIC FINDINGS

No Bones About It

Even 2,000 years after the death of King Herod, archaeologists could not find his tomb. In fact, one expert studied clues and actively searched for 35 years. Finally, in 2007, he found Herod's fancy **sarcophagus** which had been broken, probably soon after he died.

Michael Melford/National Geographic/Getty Images

Mysterious Metal

In a cave in the Judean Desert, east of Jerusalem and down to the Dead Sea, more than 400 copper objects were discovered, wrapped in a reed mat. Experts believe the objects are 6,000 years old.

Chalcolithic/The Israel Museum, Jerusalem, Israel/Collection of the Israel Antiquities Authority/The Bridgeman Art Library

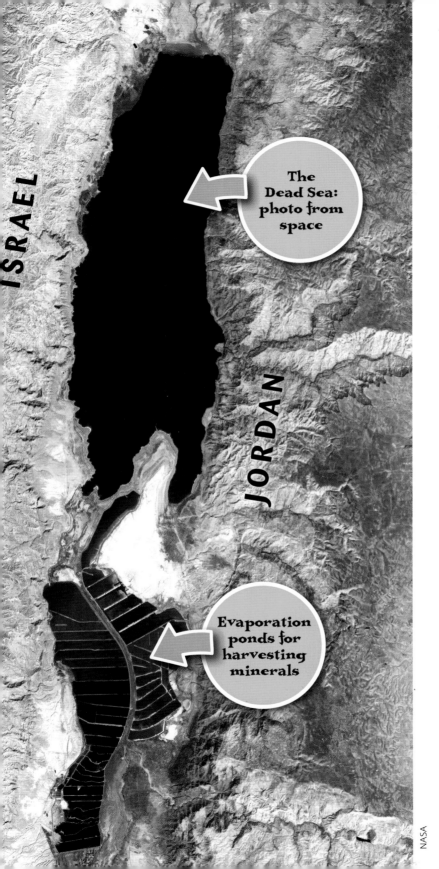

The Dead Sea: photo from space

Evaporation ponds for harvesting minerals

ISRAEL

JORDAN

Living Among the Dead

In 2010, 100 feet below the surface of the **Dead Sea**, located between Israel and Jordan, craters were discovered that are wider than a tennis court and very deep. The bigger discovery is actually much smaller— the presence of tiny, living bacteria in water that's too salty for most living things to survive—including the scientists who want to study the hardy microorganisms.

NASA

45

TERRIFIC TREASURE

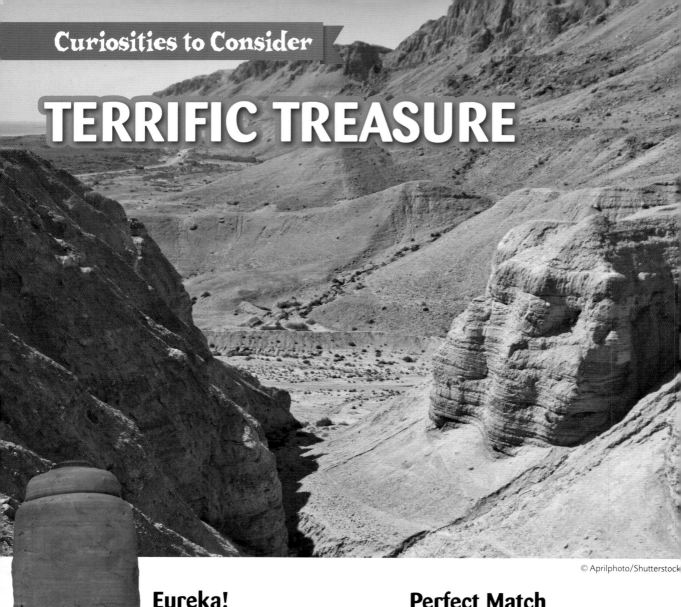

© Aprilphoto/Shutterstock

© by Zondervan

Eureka!

In 1946, shepherds made one of the greatest discoveries in history. In a cave, now called the Qumran site, inside a sealed clay jar, were seven ancient scrolls that had survived thousands of years.

Perfect Match

Before the Dead Sea Scrolls, the oldest Old Testament writings found were clay tablets from Babylon and papyri from Egypt. But these scrolls are even older—by about 1,000 years. By noticing how faithfully and carefully ancient Jews copied Scripture word-for-word, we can confirm that the modern Bibles we read today were passed on very exactly.